For all Dads, Fathers, and Daddies

Other books by Marcus Pfister
THE RAINBOW FISH
THE CHRISTMAS STAR
PENGUIN PETE
PENGUIN PETE'S NEW FRIENDS
PENGUIN PETE AND PAT
PENGUIN PETE, AHOY
HOPPER
HOPPER HUNTS FOR SPRING
HOPPER'S EASTER SURPRISE
CHRIS & CROC

First published in the United States, Great Britain, Canada,
Australia, and New Zealand in 1994 by North-South Books,
an imprint of Nord-Süd Verlag AG, Gossau Zürich, Switzerland.

Distributed in the United States by North-South Books Inc., New York.

Library of Congress Cataloging-in-Publication Data
Pfister, Marcus.
[Papa Pit und Tim. English]
Penguin Pete and Little Tim / by Marcus Pfister ; translated by Rosemary Lanning.
"First published in Switzerland under the title: Papa Pit und Tim"—T.p. verso.
Summary: While taking a walk with his father, a little penguin throws snowballs,
rides a dogsled, slides down a slippery slope, gets lost in the snow, swims with seals,
gets carried home, and asks to do it all again tomorrow.
ISBN 1-55858-301-7 (trade binding)
ISBN 1-55858-302-5 (library binding)
[1. Penguins—Fiction. 2. Fathers and sons—Fiction.
3. Walking—Fiction.] I. Lanning, Rosemary. II. Title.
PZ7.P448558Pg 1994
[E]—dc20   94-5093

A CIP catalogue record for this book is
available from The British Library.

1 3 5 7 9 10 8 6 4 2
Printed in Belgium

Penguin Pete and Little Tim

By Marcus Pfister

TRANSLATED BY ROSEMARY LANNING

North-South Books / New York / London

All night long snow had been falling, and as the sun came up, everything was quiet and still. There was no sign of a penguin family, except three heaps of snow.

Then one of the heaps began to move, and out came a bright yellow beak. It was Penguin Pete!

"Good morning, Tim," he said cheerfully to the smallest snowdrift. "Did you sleep well?"

Little Tim shook the snow from his head. "Where did all this come from?" he asked crossly.

"Never mind the snow," said Penguin Pete. "Let's go for a walk and warm up. We can let your mother sleep a little longer."

Off they went, with Pete leading the way, pushing the thick snow aside to clear a path for Tim.

Suddenly Tim shouted, "Hey, Dad, look at me!"
Pete turned around and ducked as a snowball whizzed
over his head. Pete threw back as many snowballs as
he could, but he was soon covered in snow from head
to foot.

"Enough! I surrender!" said Pete, laughing and brushing
the snow from his feathers.

    Soon they came to a small cliff. Pete quickly scrambled up and was walking on when he heard Tim shouting, "Help! Dad! I'm stuck!"

    Pete came running back, knelt down, and hauled Tim up.

    "Look at this, Tim," he said. "It's a dogsled. Sit down and I'll give you a ride."

    Tim was glad to rest his little legs for a while.

    "Hold tight, here we go!" said Pete.

Suddenly there was a terrible CRACK! and the sled broke right across the middle. Pete stopped and looked back. So that was why the sled had been left out in the snow!

Tim got off to push the back half of the sled. "Can we put it back together?" he asked.

"No, I don't think we can," said Pete, "but at least you've had a little rest, and it's all downhill from here."

Sure enough, they were now at the top of a hill, with a long slope below them.

"Watch me, Tim," said Pete. "I'll show you how to slide."

Pete whooshed down the hill. Then it was Tim's turn, but instead of sliding on his tummy, he tumbled head over heels, and rolled himself into a snowball.

"Hello, little snowman," said his father when Tim rolled to the bottom of the hill. "It's not as easy as it looks, is it?"

Pete freed Tim from his snowball and they waddled on.

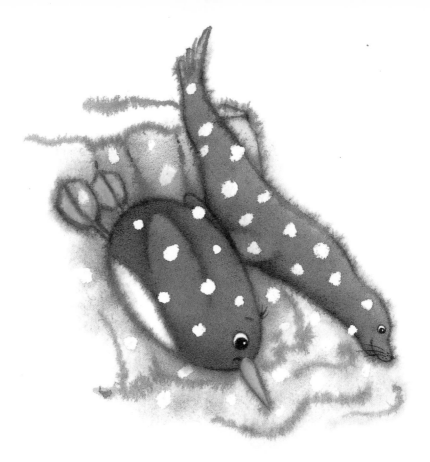

It had begun to snow again. Tim was walking very slowly through the whirling snowflakes when suddenly he realized that he couldn't see his father!

Tim stopped and called out to him, but the wind was howling so loudly, he could barely hear his own yell. Tim stood very still, and soon he was being covered with snow.

Then he heard a friendly voice. "Hello, little penguin," said a seal. "I almost missed you under all that snow. Do you want to come for a swim?"

"Oh yes, please!" said Tim. "I love swimming."

"I can't stay for long," bubbled Tim. "You see, I lost my way, and my dad always says: 'If you ever get lost, stay right where you are and I'll come and find you.'"

"So that's why you were standing as still as a snowman," said the seal.

Tim was happy swimming with the graceful seals, but he needed to get out of the water, or his father would never find him.

Tim climbed out onto the ice and waved good-bye to
his friend.
   "Stand on a rock so your father will see you," suggested
the seal as he slithered back into the sea.

Meanwhile, Pete had been looking everywhere for Tim.
He climbed a hill and shouted: "Tim, where are you?" At last
he heard a little voice answer through the swirling snow:
"Dad! I'm over here!"
"Let's go home," said Pete as he hugged Tim tightly.
"I think we've seen enough snow for today, don't you?"

"I didn't think you were ever going to find me," said Tim. "I'm so tired. Will you carry me home?"

"Of course I will," said Pete, lifting Tim onto his shoulders. "Look, Tim," he said, "the moon has come up to light our way." But there was no reply. Tim had already nodded off to sleep.

Mother Pat was waiting for them in a warm little cave, where they could shelter from the snow. Tim had woken up again, and he told his mother all about their adventures.

Then the three of them snuggled close together, and Tim murmured sleepily, "Dad, can you take me out for another walk tomorrow?"

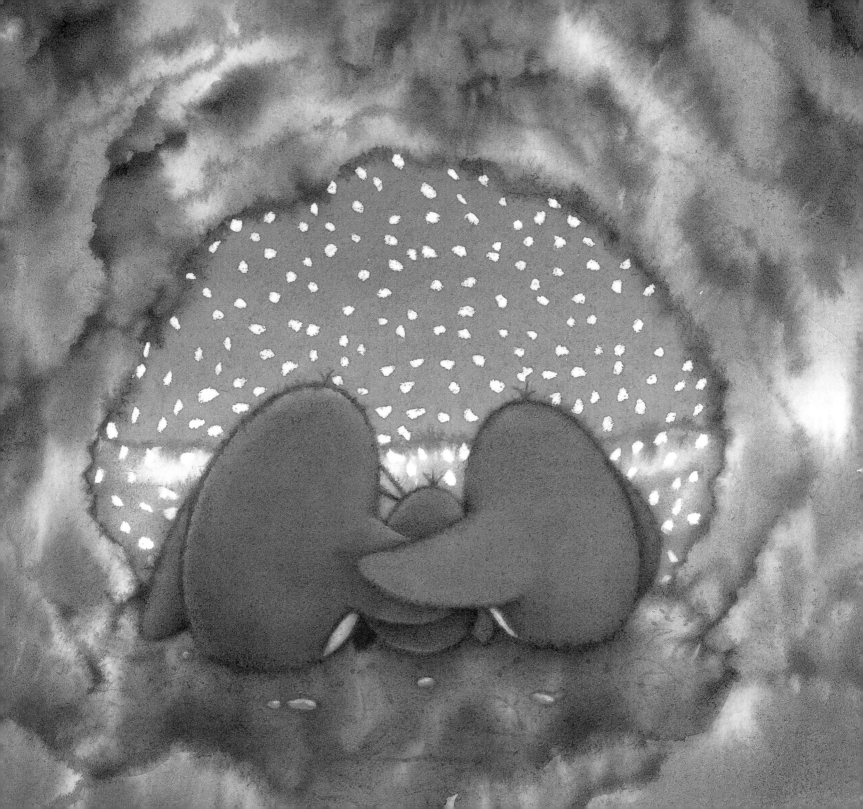